MY MUM
IS A WONDER

MY MUM
IS A WONDER

by MICHÈLE MESSAOUDI

illustrated by RUKIAH PECKHAM

THE ISLAMIC FOUNDATION

The Islamic Foundation gratefully acknowledges
Anwar Cara for the series' concept

ISBN 978-0-86037-298-1

MUSLIM CHILDREN'S LIBRARY

MY MUM IS A WONDER
Author: Michèle Messaoudi   Illustrator: Rukiah Peckham

Published by
THE ISLAMIC FOUNDATION
Markfield Conference Centre, Ratby Lane, Markfield, Leicester LE67 9SY, United Kingdom
Tel: (01530) 244944 Fax: (01530) 244946
E-mail: publications@islamic-foundation.org.uk   website: www.islamic-foundation.com

Quran House, PO Box 30611, Nairobi, Kenya

PMB 3193, Kano, Nigeria

Distributed by
Kube Publishing Ltd.
Tel: +44(0)1530 249230 Fax: +44(0)1530 249656 E-mail: info@kubepublishing.com

Printed by: IMAK Ofset, Turkey.

Every morning when I arise,
It always comes as a surprise
To see my mum dressed and ready,
Reading Qur'an by the baby.

She greets me with a smile so bright
I forget that it was ever night,
And a 'salam' that straight away
Fills me with peace for the whole day.

Her warm cuddle has the power
To get me to brave the shower.
She dries me with a hug, a kiss;
I close my eyes in pure bliss.

She helps me dress and combs my hair;
And I think: Is this really fair?
Why should I have the best of all
When some children have none at all?

Round the table we take a seat,
My mum gives us breakfast to eat;
She tells us: 'Thank Allah for food
That makes you grow and does you good'.

I thank Him too for giving me
Such a good mum and family.
'Look after mum, Allah, please do!
That's my best wish, honest and true!'

When I come home from school at four,
Whether we have one chat or more,
It puzzles me how mum can see
What's on my mind; it's beyond me!

I help my mum water and grow
Flowers and bushes, high and low;
With her I learn a seed can be
A pink one day, or a daisy.

Each time she shows me how to pray,
She reads Qur'an in such a way
That I enjoy it from the start,
And Allah's words soon reach my
heart.

She gives money to poor people,
Visits the sick in hospital;
We see friends with newborn babies
As well as lonely old ladies.

She cooks and sews to make our Eid
Happy and special, with all we need;
New clothes and toys, delicious sweets
Relatives, friends, are all my treats.

When I am sick and hot in bed,
Who stays with me and strokes my head?
Who leaves her bed for another
To comfort me, make me better?

Are you surprised that when she asks
Me to help her with a few tasks,
I never ever refuse to,
As only naughty children do?

When I grow up to be a man,
My dear mother will be a nan;
And then, who will look after her
When she gets ill and much weaker?

Why! Little me, of course, her child!
Caring for her will be my pride,
My joy, my 'thank you', o mamma,
And bring me closer to jannah.